Herobrine Revenge of a Monster

Barry J McDonald

DEDICATION

This book is dedicated to you, thank you for following my on my journey!

Chapter 1

SparkleGirl looked at her reflection in the river as she filled her bucket with water. It had been a year since the last time she'd seen Herobrine, but that had been the good Herobrine. The one that had taken her in when he didn't have to and the one who'd given her a home. But now that sweet, caring and helpful Herobrine was gone. She'd heard a rumour that he'd turned into a ghastly monster that now left destruction and death in his path.

"It's all my fault," SparkleGirl sobbed to herself and wiped away a tear. Why had she ever listened to ChuckBone? Why had she ever agreed to move into Herobrine's home, and then take it all from him the moment his back was turned? Look where that great plan had got her, killed and left to respawn back at square one with nothing to show for all her hard work. But although it felt hard for her to come to terms with what she'd lost. Herobrine had lost so much more. He'd lost his home, his favourite pet Wolfie and he'd lost himself. And she was to blame.

How could she ever make it up to him for what she had done? If Herobrine was as mad as people had said he was, how could she even say "sorry" to him? He'd probably cut her down with his sword the first second he saw her. Then even if she did try to apologise to him, how would she ever find him in this vast world. SparkleGirl pulled the bucket quickly from the river; she couldn't bear to look at her reflection a second longer. All it did was show her as a person who had sold herself out for a few possessions. She was nothing but a griefer.

Walking back to her home she wondered why she'd come back into the Minecraft world again. She could have walked away from this world and never returned. Did she really think she could just step back in time to those few happy days she'd had with Herobrine. Or had she come back to get revenge. She knew the first possibility would never happen. So maybe it was revenge that she was looking for. Not just for her, but also for Herobrine.

SparkleGirl had heard that ChuckBone and his gang had done well after

Herobrine had disappeared. After plundering Herobrine's home and taking all they needed, Chuckbone's gang had grown from strength to strength. She'd heard that he now lived in a huge fortress that was supposed to have over a hundred Minecraft players living in it. All under ChuckBone's control. ChuckBone would love all that power, SparkleGirl thought to herself. From the short time she'd known him, she could see the big ego he had. It was never enough for ChuckBone to just live and survive in Minecraft; he wanted it ALL. He wanted power and people to do his bidding.

But maybe all that was a rumour too. There were so many rumours and lies in Minecraft, who knew what the truth was anymore. Maybe that was the same as the story about Herobrine. Could someone so good really change that much and become someone so evil. If so, where would he have got all that power from? She never remembered Herobrine having magic powers before, if he had, why hadn't he used them that day when he was almost killed by a huge spider. Only for her arrow he would've died that day. So where had he got them. The only ones that practised evil magic like that were the witches. But where had Herobrine met a witch, and why would she ever give him special powers. It just didn't make sense to her.

SparkleGirl looked up from what she was doing and saw that the cubic sun was starting to lower in the sky. Having not much else to do, she took her time going back inside her home. It was peaceful at this time of day, but it also meant that the hostile mobs weren't very far either. "Time to go boy. Let's pack it in for the day," she called over to her dog. Wolfie2 ran from where he'd been sniffing the ground to join her at her homes front gate. "Having fun?" she asked. She'd never thought of taming a wolf as a pet before, but after seeing the fun and love Herobrine had for Wolfie, she decided to try it out too. It was one of the best decisions she'd made since coming back. Wolfie2 was great company and a good watch dog. Whenever there was a hostile mob close by, she always knew about it.

Like Herobrine, she'd decided to live life in Minecraft alone now. She'd been part of a group in the past and look where that had got her. Maybe Herobrine had been right. Maybe it was best to keep to yourself and not draw attention to how well you were doing. Doing otherwise would only draw griefers towards you to take everything you'd worked hard for.

As SparkleGirl switched on the booby trap at her front door, she smiled. Herobrine had taught her well in those few days they'd been together. He'd shown her his night time routine of always checking escape tunnels and making sure weapons were in plenty. This things had saved her many times. Standing in the courtyard of her home SparkleGirl looked up at the first star in the night sky and said a quick thank you. She might never see Herobrine again, but she was glad that she'd met him. Even if it had been under false pretensions. "Come on Wolfie2, I think we've some juicy pork chops with our names on them," SparkleGirl said and headed to the furnace to cook supper. "It might be a busy night, and we'll need our energy levels high. Then it's off to bed," she said, "Who knows what's going to come to our front door tonight. But whatever it is, we'll be ready for it."

After supper SparkleGirl did a quick clean up before again, checking everything was in place, and her home was safe. She'd built her home exactly as Herobrine had designed his. So she knew that it was a tough one to get into. But even tough homes could get broken into as she had seen.

Happy that everything was now in place SparkleGirl called Wolfie2 to her. "Come on boy, bedtime!" Walking to her bedroom SparkleGirl hoped she'd sleep better than she had the night before. She'd tossed and turned with a nightmare that she couldn't shake off until Wolfie2 had woken her with his barking. She hoped tonight would be a better night.

But she was wrong.

Chapter 2

"No Herobrine. Don't go. I'm sorry!" SparkleGirl screamed out before sitting up in bed. Like the night before SparkleGirl's sleep was ruined by the same horrible nightmare. In it she'd seen Herobrine standing on a hill with Wolfie by his side. On seeing her he waved to her to come join him at the top of the hill. But whenever she ran towards him, her feet would stick in strange mud that she couldn't pull free from. Then when it seemed like her feet were free at last, Herobrine would vanish from sight. SparkleGirl wiped the tears from her face and lay back down on her bed. While it could have been called a nightmare it didn't scare her. It just left frustrated that she join up with him again.

Knowing that she wasn't going to get anymore sleep, SparkleGirl got out of bed and headed to the courtyard outside. That's what I need, she thought, some fresh air and something to distract my mind. Looking around SparkleGirl smiled when she saw Wolfie2 coming over to sit by her. "Sorry boy, did I wake you? It's usually you that wakes me," she said and scratched him under the chin. "Why don't we go up top and see what the worlds like tonight?" she said walking to the stairway that led to the battlements.

Now on the highest point of her homes wall SparkleGirl and Wolfie2 looked out into the darkness. It seemed like a quiet night tonight, but that still didn't make SparkleGirl feel any better. "Maybe it's just me but I don't like this Wolfie2," SparkleGirl said and feeling for her bow. Herobrine had always told her to listen to her instincts. If something didn't seem right it was always best to be prepared. Who knew what might happen in Minecraft, it was so random living in survival mode. Then Wolfie2 growled.

SparkleGirl knew that even if her instincts were wrong, Wolfie2 never was. Her dog had protected her so many times she knew to trust him with her life. Straining her eyes to see into the blackness beyond the light of her torches SparkleGirl could see nothing. She knew this didn't mean everything was OK. She and Herobrine had had a huge battle on a quiet night like this a long time ago. One in which he'd almost lost his life. So quietness wasn't always a good thing. Then without warning, SparkleGirl spotted the first signs of movement. A spider came into view and tried to gain entry into her home over the wall. SparkleGirl let loose her first arrow and listened as the creature fell down with a satisfying crunch. Then the others came.

Out of the darkness small groups of zombies, creepers, and skeletons charged as fast as they could towards her. Taking a deep breath SparkleGirl set to her task and took out as many hostile mobs as she could. Like Herobrine had taught her, creepers could cause a problem but only if they got near your wall. Skeletons and spiders were the bigger nuisance that needed to be taken out first.

Firing off her second arrow she watched as it lifted a skeleton off its feet and sent it backwards to the ground, dead. The next skeleton SparkleGirl hit in the head, knocked its skull completely off its shoulders. “That'll teach you to mess with me!” she roared out at it and started to laugh. It probably wasn't the best time for humour, but she passed it off as either a rush of adrenaline or the excitement of action. Then things quickly became a blur of creeper, zombie, skeleton and on and on. One after another she stopped her enemies in their tracks, but they still kept on coming.

Like that night with Herobrine, something evil seemed to be out there, guiding this group of hostile mobs and sending them at her. But why, she wondered. Looking over her shoulder SparkleGirl thought about her escape tunnel. She'd built one for nights like these, maybe this was the night she'd need it. But that was a last resort, she wasn't giving up her home tonight without a fight.

Looking down SparkleGirl could see her supply of arrows were going down quickly. “Wolfie2 go get some arrows,” she called out and watched as he ran off down to the supply pile downstairs. This was a longer and harder fight than she'd been in for a long time and SparkleGirl could feel her arms getting tired from using her bow so much. Which was now a problem, as it making her arms shake and twitch and putting off her aim.

SparkleGirl smiled when she saw Wolfie2 return with a bundle of arrows in his mouth. “What would I ever do without you boy,” she asked and patted him on the head. Then taking an arrow and gripping two more in her teeth, SparkleGirl got ready to find her next target. Looking around she spotted a lone creeper who had assumed that the coast was clear and was headed towards her front gate. This one she finished off quickly with a shot to the head, followed by two more zombie kills. Now that the number of hostile mobs seemed to be getting low. SparkleGirl assumed that the fight was almost over. But she was wrong.

Just as that thought went through her mind she heard a huge explosion. "The back wall!" she screamed out in frustration. Looking back over her shoulder SparkleGirl could see a huge hole had been ripped in her wall. "Damn," she said. "Just when things had been going so well." Deciding that the fight at the front wall would have to wait. She made her back wall her priority now. Grabbing her last few remaining arrows SparkleGirl slung her bow over her shoulder and grabbed her sword. "Let's go Wolfie2," she called and ran down the stairs with Wolfie2 running closely behind her.

Trying to see through the dust and smoke, SparkleGirl could see that the hole in the wall was a large one. This would be a big repair job, but one that would have to wait until later. That's if she survived this battle. Waiting to let the dust settle, SparkleGirl could see two skeletons coming running toward the hole. "Big mistake," she said and fired one, then another arrow which hit her two targets and sent them to the ground, dead. "Better luck next time boys!" she chuckled and got ready for what was going to come next.

In didn't take long before a lone spider was attracted by all the noise and made its way to the wounded wall. This then was closely followed by three zombies and two creepers. "When is this sun ever going to come up," SparkleGirl called out in frustration looking at the night sky. The morning sun couldn't be too far away and if she could keep things as they were she might just survive. Holding her last remaining arrow in her hand, she gave it a quick kiss for luck and fired it straight into the spiders face. It proved to be a good shot that hit it straight in one eye and killed it instantly.

Looking at what had happened she was glad she'd taken out the spider first. As its body was now blocking the way for the other hostile mobs coming in through the hole. Better be quick, she thought to herself, that body's going to disappear fast. Throwing her bow to the ground SparkleGirl pulled out her sword and run as fast as she could straight towards the dead spider. Using its furry body as a platform to jump off, she leapt into the middle of the hostile mobs. On landing, SparkleGirl could see the two creepers were now getting ready to explode. Gritting her teeth she swung her sword hard and cut one creepers head off. Then stepping to the side she plunged her sword deep into the other creeper's chest. Then it was time to take care of the last three remaining zombies. SparkleGirl dispatched one zombie by chopping off its head and then killed the other two with quick stabs to their stomachs with her sword.

Stopping to look around her and catch her breath SparkleGirl's mind was in a daze. Was that it, she wondered, were there anymore on the way. Thankfully the coast looked clear now and she could she the first rays of light were beginning to come over the hill. “At last!” SparkleGirl said with relief as she watched the first of the hostile mobs begin to wander away. Now looking back at the hole in her wall. SparkleGirl realized that she'd have a busy day ahead of her with building up her home. If tonight's going to be as bad as last night, I'm really going to more need supplies, she thought.

“Wolfie2 where are you?” SparkleGirl called out and was happy to see he'd not been hurt. “Tough night wasn't it,” she said bending down to give him a big hug. Wolfie2 licked her face in response and yawned. “I'm afraid we've no time for sleep now boy. Between the damage to our wall and supplies getting low it's going to mean a visit to the village,” SparkleGirl said. “But hey it's daytime. At least nothing can go wrong. Right.”

But little did SparkleGirl know that daytime in Minecraft could be even more dangerous than night.

Chapter 3

With the sun rising high in the sky, SparkleGirl knew she'd better hurry. Although she hadn't wanted to deal with the traders in the local village, she really needed supplies in a hurry. The only problem was; the traders knew anyone coming to them needed their goods and their prices were always on the steep side. Luckily SparkleGirl had enough gold put away for times like these.

Leaving her home and walking for some time SparkleGirl and Wolfie2 eventually came to the hill that overlooked the village. Looking down she was shocked by it appearance. Where once the village was normally busy with Minecraft players chatting, bartering or selling their goods. Now it was like a ghost village. Where is everyone, SparkleGirl wondered? This wasn't the normal scene she was used to and she didn't like it. "Stay close by Wolfie2, I don't like the look of this," SparkleGirl remarked feeling for the hilt of her sword. She'd a feeling she might be needing it soon.

*****

Now at the edge of the village SparkleGirl stopped and looked ahead for any potential dangers. Even though it was daytime and no hostile mobs around the atmosphere around her still didn't feel right. As SparkleGirl walked through the village, she noticed that most of the homes and shops were smashed open and had sustained a lot of damage. What's gone on here, she wondered to herself. Taking no chances SparkleGirl pulled out her sword. If anything was going to come her way she'd was prepared to meet it. Walking slowly the two of them went through the village, all the while looking left and right to check for any sign of activity or trouble. Finally they reached the largest house in the village which was owned by a trader named BuckSeth.

BuckSeth might have gone under the name of a trader but that was misleading. Anyone meeting him for the first time would've assumed he was the most honest person you could ever meet in Minecraft. But looks could also be deceiving. There was a saying that if you ever shook BuckSeth's hand, you should always check your pockets afterwards. To sum up BuckSeth, he was nothing but a thief and a liar. But one of BuckSeth's great talents was his ability to get his hands on anything in Minecraft, even rare items. These unfortunately always came with a large price tag.

Lowering her sword SparkleGirl knocked on the door for any sign of life. As she did so the door swung open freely revealing an empty house. "You stay here boy and keep your eyes peeled," SparkleGirl said and left Wolfie2 to guard the doorway. Going inside she paused. This wasn't like BuckSeth, SparkleGirl thought to herself, leaving his home with an open door. Without warning or a noise SparkleGirl felt the cold steel of a sword at her throat. "Come to rob me SparkleGirl? Thinking of taking things that don't belong to you," a voice from behind her asked. "Well you were wrong. The others mightn't have the courage to stay put, but not me. It'll take more than, them things for me to move out of Minecraft," it sneered. "Why don't you drop that sword of yours and sit down on that chair over there in the corner."

SparkleGirl did as she was told. She knew there was no way to escape right now. It was best to play it cool. Sitting down on the stool SparkleGirl looked up to see BuckSeth standing over her with his sword in his hand. He looked bad, whatever had happened in village sure had affected him. "So what is it you're looking for SparkleGirl? An opportunity to take all you can, when no one's around." "You've got it all wrong BuckSeth. I came here looking for supplies and your shop looked like the only one open. Where's everyone gone?" SparkleGirl asked. "You must take me for a fool SparkleGirl, a smart girl like you. You knew what you were up to, coming in here. Trying to rob everything you could. Once a griefer, always a griefer!" BuckSeth sneered back.

"You've got me all wrong BuckSeth. Yes, I used to be a griefer, but those days are long behind me. I've paid for that mistake dearly and learned a painful lesson for it," SparkleGirl answered with a little anger in her voice. SparkleGirl watched as BuckSeth took all that she had said and thought it over in his mind. "So why did you come here SparkleGirl, if you're not here to help yourself to my goods?" BuckSeth asked.

"My home was overrun by hostile mobs last night. I tried my best to keep them at bay, but they got in through a damaged wall. Only for the sun coming up, I was a goner!" SparkleGirl said. "Nice story but I still don't believe you. You heard about us being attacked last night and assumed you could just walk in here and take whatever you wanted. Well you were wrong!" BuckSeth said, and waved his sword even closer to SparkleGirl's face.

SparkleGirl could see that this conversation was going nowhere. He would never believe her, and the day was moving on. She needed supplies, and she needed them quick. Better to be doing that than spending her day talking to this idiot. Then she spotted an opportunity. BuckSeth had been so busy questioning and threatening SparkleGirl that he hadn't noticed Wolfie2 come creeping up on him. Looking at the way this man was threatening his owner, SparkleGirl could see Wolfie2 was far from impressed. He was about to put the odds of this fight back into SparkleGirl's favour.

Without a sound, Wolfie2 sprang forward and sank his teeth in BuckSeth's sword arm. Immediately BuckSeth screamed out in pain and dropped his sword to the floor. Wasting no time, SparkleGirl quickly leapt from her seat and ran to where her sword was. Now turning to look at the struggle on the floor between man and dog, she could see Wolfie2 was winning. If she had had more time she probably would have let Wolfie2 soften him up a little while longer. But she didn't have the time today. "OK boy, you can let that bad man out of your mouth now. I hope you don't catch anything from that bite," SparkleGirl said. "I probably will!" BuckSeth whined back. "I wasn't talking to you I was talking to my dog. I don't care if you do catch something," Sparkle said with a chuckle "You deserve it!"

Keeping her sword trained on BuckSeth, SparkleGirl made him get up off the floor and sit on the stool she'd been on. "A bit different now the tables are turned isn't it," she said, "All you had to do was give me what I wanted, and I would've been gone by now." "I, I, I just thought you were here to rob me. Can't you see it from my point of view, an empty home so why not help yourself to everything inside? And you used to be a griefer in the past," BuckSeth said while rubbing his now sore arm. "I told you the truth, and you wouldn't believe me," SparkleGirl said lowering her sword. It looked like BuckSeth had finally got the message, and she didn't think he was a threat anymore. And anyway Wolfie2 looked like he wanted to bite him again.

"So what happened here? There used to be almost fifty players living in this village, where has everyone gone?" SparkleGirl asked BuckSeth. "It must have been the same as what happened to you last night. Out of the blue and without warning, suddenly we were overrun with hostile mobs. But these weren't the usual ones wandering around looking to cause trouble. If they were, we would have handled them easily. But no, this lot were organised. They had patterns of attack I'd never seen before. Some going one way to distract us while others came in from the other side. It didn't take long before it all became crazy here. Before we knew it some of the younger players ran for the hills. Some made it. Some didn't. The mobs were everywhere. I would have run too, but I had too much to lose, so I ran to my cellar and locked myself in there. When I came out this morning, I found it like you see now. I don't know where everyone else is; I take it they're all either dead or still running for their lives," BuckSeth said looking off in the distance.

SparkleGirl looked at BuckSeth and for almost a split second felt sorry for him. He looked really badly shook up over it all, but she didn't have time for sympathy. This day was moving too fast, and she needed supplies straight away, if she had any chance of protecting herself and her home.

Chapter 4

"OK so what have you got BuckSeth? I'll need an enchanted bow and sword at the very least, if I'm going to have any chance with those hostile mobs tonight. So I need diamonds, and I need them fast," SparkleGirl said. BuckSeth let out a sigh and replied, "Diamonds; I'm afraid no. If you're looking for wood, stone or gold. I would say OK because that's all I have. My stock ran out very fast last night. I had every Tom, Dick and Harry in here panic buying those things when those mobs came running through. In fact, I didn't even get paid for some of it!" BuckSeth said and spat on the floor.

"You're all heart you know that BuckSeth. It's just like you to be holding onto all that gold down there in your cellar hoping nobody spotted you. What a chicken," SparkleGirl answered back. She had now changed her mind about how sorry she felt for him. It was just like BuckSeth to be thinking of himself and no one else. What a worm.

"If you want diamonds you know where to find them SparkleGirl. My mine. There have been a lot of them coming back into the village lately. For whatever reason some miner found a large group of them all together. Something to do with how the land lies or whatever, it doesn't matter, but if you want diamonds that's the place to go," BuckSeth said. "Plus you know I get a cut of everything that comes out of the ground. A man has to think about his profits you know. Diamonds don't grow on trees."

"Let's get something straight BuckSeth. I'm going to that mine and I'm taking whatever I need from it. That's for payment for the way you treated me earlier," SparkleGirl said. "But my cut!" BuckSeth interrupted. "Your cut. If I have to come back here to give you a cut it will be from the edge of my sword. You lowlife," she said. "Be grateful I don't turn Wolfie2 on you again". BuckSeth looked from SparkleGirl to Wolfie2, and thought that maybe it was best to say nothing more, especially now that Wolfie2 was pulling back his lips to show his long teeth. "OK, we're even," he said. "But if you find more diamonds than you need, bring them back to me OK SparkleGirl." "In your dreams," SparkleGirl replied and headed to the door with Wolfie2 trotting along behind her.

SparkleGirl stood outside BuckSeth's home and thought about what had happened inside. Had BuckSeth been telling her the truth? He did look scared and shook up, but was he sending her into a trap. Who knew, but she had no choice if she needed diamonds she had to go to the mine. "Thanks for helping me out back there boy, you really came through for me. But the way this day is going I might need your help again," SparkleGirl said to Wolfie2. Wolfie2 smiled back as best a dog could and let out a small bark. "I love you too boy. I know you enjoyed the scuffle with BuckSeth back there. Maybe too much!" SparkleGirl said and started to laugh. "Come on let's go!"

It didn't take long before SparkleGirl could see the mine up ahead. The people of the village and area had all worked well together keeping it in good shape and well maintained. But that still didn't leave SparkleGirl feeling any better about going down there. Who knew what had happened with all those crazy hostile mobs running all over the place. For all she knew she was heading into a pit filled with spiders, zombies or creepers. Reaching down and feeling for the handle of her sword, SparkleGirl felt a little less anxious about going inside.

Stopping for a minute, SparkleGirl knelt down and gave Wolfie2 a big hug. "Before we go in here I want you to promise me something. We stick together, right. I don't want to see you get some crazy idea in your head and go running down some tunnel after a hostile mob. You hear me!" she said looking into Wolfie2 eyes. "Now don't give me those big puppy dog eyes, you do as you're told mister. Promise," Wolfie2 barked back. "You run off and I'm not coming to look for you, you hear me. OK, let's go and keep those ears of yours open," SparkleGirl said and proceeded to pull out her sword.

On entering the mine, SparkleGirl went to the nearest wall and pulled a torch off it to take with her. She knew that the front portion of the mine had been heavily worked, and she would need to go a lot deeper before she would get her hands on some diamonds. But who knew what it would be like down there. Walking along through the tunnel SparkleGirl admired how well the players had worked together to set up the mine. It was well laid out with plenty of lit torches on one wall so that you never got lost, and it also had plenty of headroom so you never had to stoop down. Then without warning Wolfie2 growled.

"What is it boy, you hear something?" SparkleGirl asked Wolfie2. SparkleGirl stopped in her tracks and listened as hard as she could. First there was nothing to be heard but after some time she could hear the familiar "plink, plink, plink" sound of someone mining up ahead. Judging by the sound there seemed to be more than one player mining their way deeper into the cave. This set SparkleGirl's mind at ease, at least she might see a friendly face down there rather than a hostile mob looking to kill her. "It sounds OK boy, but stay on your guard. You never know this lot mightn't be in a big sharing mood, so keep close to me," she said.

As she walked on, SparkleGirl started to think over her situation. Should she just sneak up and see what was ahead, which may cause the players to think that she was up to no good. Or should she just make as much noise as possible so the miners wouldn't get a fright, and know she was coming their way. When SparkleGirl heard the scream come from up ahead, she gave up on her second option and snuck up as quietly as she could to see what had happened.

Peering around the corner, SparkleGirl knew where the scream had come from. It was a player who at this moment was as dead as dead could be. That was unless you could walk around without a head on your shoulders. Then while her brain and eyes tried to register what they were seeing, she heard a second terrified scream. "Please, please don't kill me, we were told this was BuckSeth's mine. If it's your mine now, I promise I'll never come back. Here take all these diamonds," the hidden player pleaded. "I am sorr!" Then there was silence. SparkleGirl knew that that player wouldn't be mining anymore tonight. Even though she could not see what had happened, she knew he must also have had a quick death.

SparkleGirl pulled out her sword and pushed Wolfie2 back behind her. It was a miracle he hadn't opened his big mouth and barked as loud as he could. Maybe he was scared too. So what should she do now, SparkleGirl wondered. Should she crawl back quietly and try to escape, or should she attack. Thinking things over what was the worst that could happen to her. If she got killed here she would respawn back at home, albeit a damaged and weakened one with very few weapons, but she would be home again. But if she took on this mysterious killer, she might just beat them and get what she was looking for. If there were anything SparkleGirl loved, it was a challenge. Maybe it was because she liked testing herself, or maybe she was just plain stubborn. Whatever the reason SparkleGirl decided to go with plan B.

Standing up and moving out of the shadow she had been in, she could now see who the mysterious killer was. This was her worst nightmare come true. There standing in front of her was…Herobrine.

Chapter 5

It was Herobrine, and yet it was not. This was not the Herobrine she had known. The first big giveaway was his eyes, which were completely white and piercing. Long gone where the eyes she had known, to those, were they even eyes. They shone from his head just like two headlamps. And now he was coming her way, fast!

SparkleGirl held out her sword in front of her. She was sorry to see him like this, but that didn't mean she would let him attack her. Maybe she could injure him in some way to keep him from hurting her. She knew she couldn't kill her one time friend, even if she wanted to. That was even it even be done, she wondered. Whatever magic or curse was running through him now would probably make killing him a lot harder to do. Then before she could do or say anything, Wolfie2 sprang from his hiding place and stood between Herobrine and her, and let out a deep and dark growl.

Herobrine stopped in his tracks and paused. First he looked at Wolfie2 and then at SparkleGirl before looking over the two of them again. What was going on behind those eyes, SparkleGirl wondered. Then she noticed the confusion on his face. Herobrine lowered his sword, took a small step towards Wolfie2 and held out his hand. Wolfie2 pulled back his teeth and snarled; there was no way he was letting this thing come any closer to him.

SparkleGirl now knew the source of Herobrine's confusion. Whatever had happened to him albeit bad; there was still a small bit of the old Herobrine in there. The good one. "He must think Wolfie2 is his old dog. Then if he remembers that, maybe he remembers me also," she wondered. "Herobrine its SparkleGirl," SparkleGirl called to him. "It's been so long, oh Herobrine I'm so sorry for what you've become. It's all my fault. Please forgive me! I know there is good in there somewhere, you don't have to be this monster. Let me help you please!" she pleaded. Herobrine looked at SparkleGirl with a look of confusion and sadness on his face. Then when she thought he finally was remembering her again. He raised his sword, pointed it at her, and then disappeared.

"No Herobrine, please stay!" SparkleGirl begged to the now empty place where Herobrine had stood. SparkleGirl dropped to her knees and started to cry. "Oh God, what have I done. It's all my fault; it's all my fault," she cried out and started to pound the ground with her fist. SparkleGirl stayed in that shocked state a little while until a soft wet nose followed by a big wet tongue, licked her face and brought her out of her trance. "Thanks boy, I needed that," SparkleGirl said before again sobbing, quietly into Wolfie2 warm, soft fur.

Drying her eyes now, SparkleGirl knew what she must do. It was because of her and that "ChuckBone" that Herobrine had ended up like this. So it was up to her to make this better. But how. Could what had happened to him be reversed, was it possible to get the old Herobrine back, SparkleGirl wondered. She knew one thing, if she couldn't bring back Herobrine she'd do something almost as good. Get revenge for what had happened to him, and that meant paying a visit to ChuckBone. Thinking it over, that sounded like a good idea but who would know where a low life like ChuckBone lived. Minecraft was a big world and where would she start looking.

"BuckSeth," she exclaimed. "Yes, all those lowlifes hung around in the same circles. BuckSeth would probably know of ChuckBone's location." Feeling better now that she was doing something instead of wallowing in her tears, SparkleGirl got up off the ground. "Looks like we're going back to the village Wolfie2. We have to pay BuckSeth a little visit. But before that, let's get those diamonds first. I'm going to need an enchanted bow and sword even more now."

Standing outside the mine and breathing in the fresh evening air, helped clear SparkleGirl's head. She was glad to have gotten out of that mine. But now she had another problem, the sun was beginning to set and going all the way back home wasn't an option anymore. Like it or not, she would have to stay in the village with BuckSeth tonight. This was not a night she was looking forward to. "Come on Wolfie2, we have a lot of ground to cover and little light to guide the way," SparkleGirl said. Then making sure everything was secured in place she slung her bag over her shoulder and set off running at a steady jogging pace.

By the time SparkleGirl had reached the edge of the village, the sun was completely gone, and darkness had settled in. There wasn't much time to waste especially if this village was going to be overrun again tonight. SparkleGirl hoped BuckSeth had a crafting table because she would need it as soon as possible. Pulling her sword out she ran straight to his house, this time she was going to be prepared for whatever came at her. Whether that was a hostile mob or BuckSeth. There was no way he was going to get the jump on her this time. But then again after the fight with Wolfie2, he might think better of trying any trickery.

"Open up BuckSeth!" SparkleGirl roared, banging the handle of her sword on his door. "I know you're in there so don't try to ignore me. If you don't open this door in the next 10 seconds I'm breaking a window and sending Wolfie2 in there to find you". "OK, OK, I'm coming just keep that mutt away from me!" BuckSeth pleaded coming to the door. "You promise you're not here to kill me SparkleGirl. I thought we parted as friends," BuckSeth asked through a crack in the door. "I promise, but if you leave me waiting out here any longer I might just change my mind!" SparkleGirl replied and winked to Wolfie2.

Opening the door, BuckSeth didn't look any better than when she had seen him earlier. "Are you alone?" he asked nervously, as she walked past him into his home. "Where are the others? Any sign of any villagers coming back? What about the mine, did you get what you wanted? I promise if anything happened to you, it had nothing to do with me. Is that why you're here?" BuckSeth asked. "Don't worry I'm on my own. The only ones I saw were two players robbing from your mine. But they won't be doing any more mining for a while," SparkleGirl replied. "You killed them? "No, not me BuckSeth, something a lot, lot worse. Let's just say I know that the killer has no connection with you. In fact, it has a lot more to do with me, and my past," SparkleGirl replied. "But enough of the chit chat BuckSeth I need a crafting table and I need one right now. Where is it?" she asked spilling out her diamonds onto a table beside her.

BuckSeth led SparkleGirl to his enchanting table in the back of his home and stood back to let her get on with her work. "If I were you I wouldn't be just standing around here watching me. Put your eyes to better use and look out the front windows. If those things are going to come racing through here I want to know about it right away," SparkleGirl said waving BuckSeth away with her hand.

As SparkleGirl set to work on the enchanting table to create her new sword and bow, she stopped for a moment. Working on the table brought her back to the time when Herobrine had shown her how to use a crafting table. Good old Herobrine, he hadn't noticed that that she already knew all the crafting recipes already. He had just presumed that she was a quick learner. BuckSeth's voice broke her from her daydream, "Quick, they're coming they're coming" he squealed. Working quickly SparkleGirl combined all the ingredients of the recipe and smiled when she saw what she had created. "Showtime!" she whispered to herself and then ran to the front windows to see what the hostile mobs had in store for them.

Whatever it was going to be, she would be ready for it.

Chapter 6

Just as SparkleGirl reached the front window the first explosion rang out, followed by two further ones at the other end of the village. "What weapons have you got here, please say you're well equipped?" she asked BuckSeth. "Other than a handful of arrows, a sword and some booby traps not much else," he replied. "Damn! Can I count on you in a fight BuckSeth, or am I going to find myself fighting alone?" BuckSeth blushed at that remark. "Just as I thought. It looks like it's just you and me Wolfie2," SparkleGirl said looking at her dog.

"Now before you think about running out on me, I need some information that you have. Where can I find ChuckBone?" SparkleGirl asked turning to face BuckSeth. BuckSeth looked back with a blank expression on his face. "Never heard of him," he replied. "Wrong answer BuckSeth. You can either tell me now, or I can have Wolfie2 chew on you for a while. So where is ChuckBone?" "I don't know, I've never heard of him SparkleGirl," BuckSeth replied rather too quickly for SparkleGirl's liking. "Wolfie2 show the nice man your teeth, I don't think he got a good enough look the last time you met, give him a smile boy."

Wolfie2 was only too happy to oblige and pulled back his lips to reveal two sets of very long and very sharp white teeth. "OK, OK, I'll tell you! He has a place somewhere up North from here. It's almost a four day ride away. Look, I've not dealt with him personally, so whatever he did on you it has nothing to do with me, you hear me. Now call that mutt off!" BuckSeth pleaded and tried to put a chair between himself and Wolfie2. "You wouldn't lie to me now, would you BuckSeth? Because I can come back here if you're lying to me," SparkleGirl said. "I promise, I promise, why would I, you have my word!" "Well that's okay. Now let's try to sort out this little mess outside", she said and walked back to look out the window again.

As she had feared, this was not a small number of hostile mobs just wandering around. Someone was out there again guiding them. But why, the village was almost empty now other than the three of them in BuckSeth's house. So why go back through the village again. Maybe this was a statement, whoever was behind it was looking to show the Minecraft players that they weren't to be messed with.

"OK, have you got somewhere high up, I could use a high position to use my bow right now. I can pick off some of them with whatever arrows we've left. Then unfortunately, it's all going to be a hand to hand sword fight after that," SparkleGirl said turning around. "Go to my attic, I have a trapdoor that opens onto the roof," BuckSeth said. "I made it as an escape route in case I ever needed it. Once you're on the roof, you'll find a small stairway that leads down to the ground." "Are you coming with me or do you fancy your chances here on your own BuckSeth?" SparkleGirl asked already making her way to the stairs that lead to the first floor.

SparkleGirl never got an answer to that question because as soon as her back was turned BuckSeth disappeared. Probably gone to his cellar, she thought. "Looks like it's just you and me boy. Come on let's teach these hostile mobs that they can't mess with us and get away with it." Wolfie2 barked happily and ran ahead up the stairs.

Looking down from the roof, SparkleGirl could see the situation better. Off to one side of the village some smoke was rising from a burnt out house, and on the other side a fire looked like it was spreading from one building to another. SparkleGirl pulled out her new bow and felt the weight of it in her hand. It felt good to have a fine weapon like this and she couldn't wait to try it out.

It didn't take long before the first hostile mob came into sight; a lone creeper slowly shuffling along with no target in mind. SparkleGirl took out an arrow, placed it in her bow and took aim. Her new bow gave out a satisfyingly "ping" sound as the arrow left on its way to its target. The arrow hit the creeper full in the chest and sent it crashing to the ground, dead. SparkleGirl smiled; this bow was ever better than she thought and she couldn't wait for the next mob to come into sight. As SparkleGirl watched from above, she could just make out how the hostile mobs were working, making sure each building was empty before moving onto the next. Who could be in charge, she wondered, someone must be out there watching how its minions were doing and directing them to the next area to look. But who could it be and where were they. By now SparkleGirl eyes were more accustomed to the dark, and she squinted to see where the leader could be.

Then she spotted him, Herobrine.

Although at first in the shadows, she could see his two glowing eyes looking left and right admiring his handy work. "What again, what's were the chances of meeting him twice in one day," SparkleGirl said to herself. Now everything made sense to her. The increase in hostile mobs in the area, Herobrine, they were all connected. It was as if he were a magnet drawing anything evil to him and then using it for his purpose. This had to stop. SparkleGirl threw her bow over her shoulder and raced down the stairway to the ground below with Wolfie2 coming behind her.

On the way down SparkleGirl wondered what she would do. What could she say to him that would make him stop, was there any way she could reason with this one time friend. Then before she would be able to get anywhere near him, SparkleGirl would need to cut a way through his evil mobs. Taking her bow off her shoulder and grabbing two arrows, she placed one in her bow and clenched the other one between her teeth. Now better prepared, she ran at the first mob she saw, which was a creeper, and finished him off with a quick arrow to the head. Then almost immediately she fired another shot into a skeleton's ribcage and sent him to the ground. For those two to three seconds she had a moment of surprise before every other hostile mob in the area saw what had happened and came running at her.

Down to her last few arrows SparkleGirl tried to do as much damage as she could. She could handle zombies and spiders easily using her sword, but things like skeletons and creepers were safer killed with a bow and arrow. Working to her plan, SparkleGirl sized up her enemies before quickly picking out a spider and two skeletons that she could get rid of. Then taking very little time, she moved quickly from target to target and dispatched the three of them one after another. Now out of arrows she quickly threw down her bow and pulled out her sword.

Glad that she now had an enchanted sword, SparkleGirl easily chopped her way through the first group of hostile mobs that came at her. One creeper lost a head before he tried to explode, and two zombies met a quick death, one stabbed in the stomach, and another losing both of his legs. But it was not over. Slowly the word got through the ranks of hostile mobs that someone was doing great damage to their group, and they all started to come her way. As SparkleGirl fought on, she knew that she was starting to lose this battle, not for lack of skill, but due to her energy level which was starting to go down. Swinging an enchanted sword was tiring work.

"HEROBRINE IF YOU CAN HEAR ME, CALL THESE THINGS OFF, ITS ME SPARKLEGIRL. STOP THIS, THERE'S NO NEED TO DO THIS, I MEAN YOU NO HARM. PLEASE HEROBRINE, PLEASE!" SparkleGirl screamed at the top of her voice. Then just when she thought her message hadn't got through, the hostile mobs stopped their advance and moved apart. This left Herobrine a clear path to walk through the group.

What was going to happen next, SparkleGirl didn't know.

Chapter 7

Now that SparkleGirl had a better chance to look at her friend's face she could see it wasn't him anymore. Long gone was the face that was prone to smiling, now it was replaced by a mask that just looked frozen. Meeting someone like that would have been scary enough, she thought, but those "eyes" if you could call them that, just shone like two suns in his head. In a way, she felt like he could see right through her. There has to be some small bit of the old Herobrine in there, SparkleGirl thought to herself. Maybe locked away in a part of his brain that she could reach. It might just take a little prizing to get it free. Could he really be all monster, SparkleGirl didn't believe so. He had let her escape earlier in the day hadn't he? Maybe this proved that there was still some good in him.

SparkleGirl wondered what was going on in Herobrine's head right now; it was hard to tell. Usually you could read what someone was thinking by the look on their face or how their eyes were. But not with him. How could anyone read a face like that, or those eyes. They were just two burning pools of light. "Let me help you Herobrine, let me try to make you better. I don't know how, but I will travel the lengths of Minecraft to find someone with a cure, please let me help you! If anyone's to blame for what happened to you it's me and ChuckBone," SparkleGirl pleaded.

How had she ever fallen for ChuckBone's idea? She hated herself for having gone into Herobrine's home only to turn around and rob him of everything. BuckSeth was probably right about her, once a griefer always a griefer. "You never met ChuckBone but he was the one that sent me to trick you out of your home, and… he also was the one that… killed me… and Wolfie," SparkleGirl said. It was a painful memory she didn't like to dwell on. On remember all of this, a small tear started to roll down SparkleGirl's cheek. At this Herobrine took a step towards her. Automatically SparkleGirl took a step backwards, was she in danger of getting hurt she wondered.

Watching Herobrine come towards her, she feared the worst until he placed his hand softly on her cheek. Not knowing what to do next, SparkleGirl held it there and said slowly and softly, "I'm so very sorry for everything Herobrine. Can you ever forgive me?" She looked into his face for any sign of response but got nothing. "You remember me don't you? You remember those fun times we had together; you do, don't you?" SparkleGirl could almost feel her heart start to break, what had Herobrine gone through since the last time she'd seen him. She wasn't sure but looking at him now; it must have been painful. Why would anyone go through this willingly to become a monster like this, it just didn't make sense.

Herobrine turned to look down at Wolfie2 who had no idea what he should do. "It's OK boy; this was a friend of mine," SparkleGirl said. She thought it better to say "was" rather than "is" because she really wasn't sure anymore. Things could never go back to the way they used to be, and she must face that fact now. But there was one thing she could do, she might not be able to change the past but she could change the present and the future. ChuckBone was going to pay for this, she didn't know how she was going to find him but she would surely try. "I'll make ChuckBone and his group pay for what they did to you, Wolfie and me." SparkleGirl said to Herobrine.

As she said this, SparkleGirl could see the fire in Herobrine's eyes blaze brighter than before, and she stepped back from him afraid. Whatever had happened SparkleGirl didn't know. Was it an old memory that he suddenly remembered. Whatever it was, SparkleGirl thought it looked like Herobrine now had his mind fixed on revenge. Then stepping back from her, Herobrine took a moment to look at SparkleGirl once more before suddenly vanishing. As he did so, all the hostile mobs that surrounded SparkleGirl and Wolfie2 suddenly turned and walked away. Whatever fight that was in them before was now gone.

SparkleGirl stood in place for a few moments to try to process what she had seen. It was beyond doubt now, that Herobrine had the power to control hostile mobs at will. All those stories she'd heard in the past and thought were exaggerations were now true. He had indeed become a monster, how, she didn't know. But was he one hundred percent bad, was there no sign of the old Herobrine in there. He could have easily walked away and let his mobs do his dirty work but he hadn't. Then from the way he looked at her before he disappeared, she wondered if Herobrine really had his mind set on revenge. That thought stayed for a while in

SparkleGirl's mind before a voice from behind woke her from her thoughts.

"Are they gone? What happened, what did he say to you? Who was that, was that Herobrine? Are the two of you working together?" BuckSeth asked, firing off one question after another. "I was right, there is something bad about you. I thought you were just a griefer at first but now this, wait until everyone hears about this!" BuckSeth continued. On hearing BuckSeth's last comment, SparkleGirl was filled with rage and she ran at him. Pulling back her sword, SparkleGirl swung it hard and hit BuckSeth on the side of the head with it. Instantly BuckSeth fell to the ground and rolled around in pain holding his head. "The next time I'll not hit you with the flat of my sword, you toad. I'll be taking your head off your shoulders. You coward, you ran at the first sign of trouble and left me to defend this place. I hope it burns to the ground, and you burn with it. Oh and by the way, I need a horse. I see you've a fine one tied up in your stable. Think of it as payment for saving your miserable hide," SparkleGirl said and headed in the direction of BuckSeth's stable.

As she threw a saddle over BuckSeth's horse, SparkleGirl wondered to herself. What if she were wrong about what the expression on Herobrine's face had meant. What if he were not looking for revenge against ChuckBone. Then again if he were, what could she offer him in a fight. He would have all those hostile mobs at his control; she had nothing but a sword and a bow. What good would that be? SparkleGirl knew at least one thing right now, going back to her home was not the best decision to make. She had now seen up close what ChuckBone's griefing and trickery had caused and she couldn't let this go. Herobrine had lost everything because of him and she was going to make him pay for it. She hoped Herobrine wouldn't get there first, because she wanted to see him take ChuckBone's world apart with her own eyes.

Chapter 8

SparkleGirl had ridden BuckSeth's horse hard for the first two days of her journey. She wanted to get to ChuckBone's home as soon as possible, this was one fight she didn't want to miss. SparkleGirl felt sorry that she had to push BuckSeth's horse hard like this. It was punishment enough to have had carry BuckSeth's fat body around on its back, without all this extra work that she was now giving it. Looking down at Wolfie2 from high up on her saddle, she could see he was feeling the strain of the fast pace also. "Just one more day boy and our journey will be at an end," SparkleGirl said. Pausing for a moment SparkleGirl thought over what she had just said, the end might be coming in more ways than she imagined.

Although the past two nights had been virtually hostile mob free. SparkleGirl still dug herself a deep pit each night to protect herself and Wolfie2. For her horse, she made a temporary fence each night to keep it from running away. But there was little chance of that. By the time each evening had come, all three of them were too exhausted to do any wandering around and rest was in the forefront of all of their minds. But though the nights were quiet she could still feel like someone was out there watching her every move. This feeling she put to the back of her mind as just tiredness or an overactive mind. Surely Wolfie2 would have picked up on the scent of a stranger and let her know about it, SparkleGirl thought.

"It's starting to get dark boy, let's set up camp for the night. That looks like a good place to stop, over there by that cliff. At least we'll have some protective cover behind us to keep hostile mobs at bay," SparkleGirl said pointing the way. Wolfie2 looked up at SparkleGirl and in his own doggy way, nodded his head in agreement. A rest was welcomed as far as he was concerned. Leaping down from her horse SparkleGirl took in her surroundings. This looked like a good place to settle for the night she thought. There were a few trees around that should could use to make some arrows and a wooden fence for her horse. Looking up at the sky, she could see the sun was beginning to make its downward journey so there was no time to lose. "Let's tie you up here… horse," SparkleGirl said to BuckSeth's horse. She had to stop calling him that, she thought. So what name could she give it? He was fast and strong, so maybe "LightFoot," yes that sounded like a decent name.

"Lightfoot, do you like that name fella?" SparkleGirl asked patting the horse on the neck. BuckSeth's horse let out a snort of approval which seemed to answer her question. "Lightfoot is it then.Wolfie2 I want you to meet Lightfoot, LightFoot this here is Wolfie2 and I'm SparkleGirl," she said with a chuckle. If anyone had heard her they would have presumed she'd lost her mind, but she didn't care. SparkleGirl loved animals, and she would happily spend hours talking to them. The animals in Minecraft had never caused her any problems it had been the people that were the ones to watch out for.

Leaving Wolfie2 with Lightfoot at their new campsite, SparkleGirl headed to the nearest trees and started to chop them with her iron axe. Although she was tired and in need of a meal she wanted to get this work out of the way. Then she could relax and get herself and Wolfie2 sorted for the night. Deep in thought about the battle ahead and what she may or may not be able to do in the fight, she never heard a stranger come up behind her."So SparkleGirl we finally meet," a voice spoke from behind her. SparkleGirl jumped and turned both in fright and readiness to see who had crept up behind her. Looking firstly like a villager, SparkleGirl was shocked to find herself face to face with a witch. "What!" SparkleGirl said gripping her sword handle tightly and getting ready to swing it. But before she had another chance to say or do anything, she felt her body being covered in a potion that was thrown by the witch. Then everything started to go in slow motion. SparkleGirl raised her sword as best she could and swung it at the witch with no success. The witch easily side stepped the sword and moved into a safer position. SparkleGirl then knew she was in big trouble.

In all her time in Minecraft, SparkleGirl hadn't come upon many witches. Those that she had met she killed easily from a safe bow and arrow distance. This was going to be a whole new kind of fight altogether. SparkleGirl tried to shake the slowness from her body but to no avail; it felt like her hands just weren't getting the message from her brain anymore. She now knew she had been attacked with a slowness potion, and there was very little she could do about it.

"We could do this all night SparkleGirl. You, swinging your sword wildly and I moving out of the way. What say we quit this little charade and you give up? But before I kill you I want to know, how have you got such a hold over Herobrine? It was because of you that I got him to take that potion in the first place and become, well, the beautiful monster that he now is. But now you've ruined it all. Sending him to ChuckBone to get his revenge. You really have thrown a spanner in the works this time madam and set both my minions up against each other," the witch said. "What! ChuckBone's working for you too," SparkleGirl announced in amazement. "Yes, SparkleGirl, I didn't want to rely on just one evil character in Minecraft to do my bidding. It's more fun with two don't you think. Both doing the same job but on different ends of the scale. Herobrine attacking all those Minecraft players and ruining their little games and then ChuckBone on the other side, taking and griefing as much as he wants. It's a fabulous plan don't you think." The witch smiled under her large drooping nose.

"But why. Why do this, what will you ever gain by destroying everyone in Minecraft?" SparkleGirl asked in confusion. "Nothing, not a single thing. But that's not what I want; I want you all out of here. This land used to be our world until you people started coming in here, building homes, robbing our mines and mountains of gold and diamonds. None of it was yours to take, but that didn't stop you. GRIEFERS YOU ALL ARE, EVERY SINGLE ONE OF YOU!" the witch screamed pointing at SparkleGirl.

Taking a moment to get her composure the witch continued, "And my plan was going so well, until you had to come back into Minecraft and show your face to Herobrine. Now whatever power I used to have over him is now weakened, and he is hell bent on taking ChuckBone down. This I can't let happen. I can't let them both kill each other and leave me back at square one. That won't happen. This is one of the reasons I'm here with you sweet SparkleGirl, to tidy up a loose end. I can't have you in this world distracting my greatest creation with whatever it is you have over him. Say goodbye!" the witch said and pulled another potion from under her cloak.

SparkleGirl looked at the vial of potion and smiled. This could be the end for her, but she wasn't going without a fight. Raising her sword, she half-heartedly swung at the witch and missed. But she didn't care; she could see what was coming. Just as the witch was about to let go of the vial, she screamed. Being so busy bragging about her creations and focused on killing SparkleGirl, the witch hadn't seen Wolfie2 coming up behind her. Like his previous attack on BuckSeth, Wolfie2 had lunged and grabbed onto the witch's arm, which he was now tearing at it with teeth. Losing her grip on the mystery vial it fell softly to the ground, whereupon SparkleGirl kicked it far from her reach.

Looking at the witch screaming for mercy, SparkleGirl knew what she had to do. This had been the witch that had made Herobrine the monster that he had become. There was no way she could let her escape. She also knew she couldn't let the witch stop Herobrine getting his revenge on ChuckBone. Shaking off the last effects of the slowness potion, she gripped her sword handle tightly and brought it down as hard she could, and sliced through the witch's neck.

Chapter 9

"That's enough boy; she's dead. You can let go now," SparkleGirl said while catching her breath. How stupid she'd been to have let a witch come walking up on her like that. That had been too close for comfort. If Wolfie2 hadn't saved her when he did, she didn't know what would have happened. Would she have respawned back after that attack, or would she have been permanently out of the game forever. She thought it would probably be the latter. Whatever that witch was looking to do, she sure wouldn't want SparkleGirl back in the Minecraft world meddling in her plans again.

SparkleGirl now finally knew what had happened to Herobrine. He had been a helpless pawn in the witch's game and never known it. The witch knew how good a player Herobrine was, and all she needed was a way to get him to change sides and come over to her way of thinking. That's where SparkleGirl had come into the plan; she had been a small cog in a larger machine that she knew nothing about. But ChuckBone did, he knew everything because he was promised free rein to do whatever he wanted to do. DAMN YOU CHUCKBONE! SparkleGirl shouted to the sky, "You better pray that Herobrine gets you first you SCUM!"

SparkleGirl searched the ground where the witch had fallen in case she'd dropped anything. Other than some gunpowder and a few spider eyes, there was very little left that she could use. "If only the witch had dropped something useful like a healing or swiftness potion that would have come in handy boy," SparkleGirl said scratching her dog behind the ear. "You did it again and saved my life. What would I ever do without you by my side? You deserve the biggest steak I can find for what you did today. Unfortunately, it's going to be cooked pork chops again tonight. Maybe when we get to ChuckBone's we can treat ourselves to something nice." Wolfie2 licked his lips when he heard the word "steak" mentioned and barked in agreement.

Walking back to where she had planned to set up camp, SparkleGirl considered her options. ChuckBone's lair was only a day's ride away but if she left now she could get there a lot sooner. Of course traveling at night would be slow, and there may be more dangers. But after what she'd gone through with the witch, SparkleGirl didn't think you would face anything as bad as that again tonight. Patting her horse Lightfoot lightly on the neck, she apologised for what she was about to do. "I'm sorry Lightfoot but I don't want to be hanging around this place any longer than I need to. Who knows what else may come at us now." While they all needed the rest right now, SparkleGirl knew that travelling at night would be slower on everyone and not as exhausting. They could sleep when they got near ChuckBone's, she hoped.

Traveling through the night wasn't as bad as SparkleGirl had thought it would be. For whatever reason the hostile mobs in the area were gone, but were they. Rather than gone maybe they were being redirected elsewhere. To SparkleGirl this looked like Herobrine's work; he must be building an army and pulling every mob he could to him. Looking skyward she could see that the sky was starting to lighten, sunrise wouldn't be too far away and another day.

After two more hours of traveling she saw what she'd been looking for. There in the distance was a huge fortress, one of the largest ones she'd ever seen. ChuckBone, it had to be his. Getting a little closer now, SparkleGirl admired the large towers that grew tall from the ground and the high wall that joined them together. This home was going to be incredibly hard to break into, and she didn't envy Herobrine's job. But if anyone could do this, it was him. SparkleGirl just hoped that Herobrine still had all the knowledge and wisdom from his past life inside of him. He would need it.

"You have reached your destination," SparkleGirl said out loud and chuckled. Wolfie2 turned when he heard this and cocked his head to the side. "Sorry boy you wouldn't understand," she said with a smile. "It's time to make camp and get some rest. I don't think anything will happen to us during the day."

Moving back a bit to put some distance between herself and the fortress, SparkleGirl picked a suitable place on a hill. It was far enough away she thought and gave her a better view to see what was happening below. "OK Lightfoot, there's some nice grassland over there, you go and enjoy yourself!" she said guiding her horse. "OK Wolfie2, let's get our heads down for the day. I'm beat, and I'm pretty sure you are too," SparkleGirl said trying to hold back a yawn. "Maybe I should dig a shallow pit for us over there. It can give us some cover and help to keep us hidden in case anyone goes by."

Digging quickly, SparkleGirl made a pit which was big enough for herself, Wolfie2 and her belongings. A bed could come later and some food. Thinking over those things in her mind, she quickly fell fast asleep and into a world of dreams and nightmares. In one nightmare, she was like a rubber toy that was being stretched two ways. ChuckBone on one side pulling her to him and Herobrine pulling the other way, each one trying hard to get her to their side. In another dream, she woke up with a witch's mask on her face but try as she might she couldn't pull it free. Tossing and turning she woke herself up with a scream. Then sitting up to catch her breath she looked around to find herself in another nightmare, but this time she was wide awake.

"Hello sleepy head, it's so good to see you again. How long has it been SparkleGirl?" Without turning her head, SparkleGirl knew the owner of the voice. No, it couldn't be true, she thought to herself. But now looking around her she found herself surrounded by ChuckBone and his gang.

"Grab her!" Chuckbone cried.

Chapter 10

As SparkleGirl was being led away, she thought about what had gone wrong with her plan. It had seemed a good one at the time, but thinking it over now; it had been made with a tired brain. She had never taken into consideration that Wolfie2 might get up and go for a walk, and leave her without any warning of incoming intruders. She also hadn't taken into consideration how one of ChuckBone's patrols might have spotted Lightfoot on the hill grazing, and come to have a closer look. She probably should have put a roof over her pit as added cover, but wrongly assumed that since it was daytime she wouldn't need it.

"Take her to our cells," ChuckBone called out to one of his henchmen. "SparkleGirl I'm sorry that we must part for now, but I have more important matters to look at. Don't worry there will be plenty of time to talk about old times." ChuckBone sneered and walked away with a small group of players. As he went SparkleGirl couldn't help but hear ChuckBone's last conversation with another player, "You mean all the hostile mobs in the area have disappeared, but where have they gone?" "I don't know ChuckBone it beats me, but I don't like it. I've a funny feeling something bad is about to happen." SparkleGirl smiled to herself, if only they knew. She hoped ChuckBone wouldn't kill her just yet, because things were going to get very interesting around here.

Getting closer to ChuckBone's fortress SparkleGirl had to admire it. It was big and looked strong but looks could also be deceiving. This home had been made by a person who thought he had nothing to fear in Minecraft, he had a witch by his side so what could go wrong. Looking closer now she could see that this confidence had left his fortress lacking some things. Firstly the walls were high but had no overhang, this left them open to an attack from spiders. Then she could see there were some blind spots where anyone on the wall couldn't see what was coming at them. The height of the wall was also a design problem, sure it looked impressive, but it was also a long distance to shoot down from. If Chuckbone had players with very little battle experience, there were bound to be a lot of missed shots.

When she made in through the main gate, SparkleGirl was lead to a huge courtyard with lots of players coming and going. Looking closely, she spotted some of ChuckBone's older players stop what they were doing and look over at her. "Great to see you too guys, great to be back!" SparkleGirl shouted over with sarcasm in her voice. "I'm a bit tied up at the moment but maybe we could get together later, and I could run a sword through you," SparkleGirl said with a chuckle. She had a few favours to hand out to "old" friends and hoped she would break free later to do it.

"So where are we going guys? What does big bad ChuckBone have in mind for me, a prison cell?" she asked. "I hope it's good and strong, you might want to join me. It could be a lot safer in there, than out here when things start to go down." SparkleGirl laughed when she saw the confusion on the players faces. "Oh, you don't know. Well I won't spoil the surprise for you but I know you'll love it. At least I hope you do," she said and laughed again.

One player panicked, pulled out his sword and put it to SparkleGirl's throat. "I could kill you right here, what do you think of that?" he said with a sneer "Then you'll see how funny things are." "That's fine do it if you must, but I wouldn't. I don't think ChuckBone would be too happy if that happened while he was away. And you might need my help later," SparkleGirl said back with a smile. Angry now that there was nothing he could do, the player swung his sword and hit SparkleGirl with the flat of it to the side of her head, knocking her out cold.

When SparkleGirl woke up, her head was throbbing from the blow. Touching the spot softly she could feel a lump where the sword had hit. She'd probably deserved it for her teasing, but that still didn't make her head feel any better. Another one to add to my list, she thought. Sitting on the floor in the corner of her cell, SparkleGirl wondered what the time was, was it getting dark. Then another shocking thought came to her. With all her bragging and bravado she'd completely forgotten about Wolfie2. Was he still alive she wondered, or had ChuckBone got his hands on her dog too? "I have to get out of here," SparkleGirl said to herself, and walked around her cell to see if she could find any weaknesses. There were none. Her only chance of escape now was when her jailer came to see how she was doing, or when she was being taken to see ChuckBone. Then she could strike.

SparkleGirl lay on the floor of her cell and thought about the situation she now found herself in. ChuckBone or whoever had created these cells had tried to give the smallest amount of space as punishment, but there was a flaw in that thinking. SparkleGirl moved her body until she was lying crossways in her cell, then stretching her hands above her head and stretching her legs out. She found she could easily touch the walls opposite each other. What she was about to do next would be difficult but what else could she do stuck in here?

Pushing hard against both walls with her hands and feet, SparkleGirl moved off the floor and travelled up towards the ceiling. Next would come the tricky part. It would be hard to hold herself up against the ceiling for any long length of time. "HELP ME, HELP ME!" she screamed at the top of her voice. SparkleGirl knew anyone hearing those words were bound to come running, even if they were not intent on helping, curiosity would get the better of them, and they would want to see why she was crying out.

On cue, the cell door opened slowly, and a player poked his head in. Now confused to find an empty cell, he flung the door wide open and ran into the middle of the room looking for his captive. SparkleGirl knew she'd need to be quick, it was only a matter of time before he looked up and spotted her. Not waiting a second longer, SparkleGirl let gravity do its work, and she let go. As she fell she pulled her two knees into her stomach, curled into a tight ball and braced herself for impact.

As she had suspected the player was not ready for an attack from above, so when she crashed into him her weight sent him flying into the far wall with a "crunch"! She knew from the sound he wouldn't be getting up after that fall. Hopefully he was unconscious and not dead; the last thing she needed right now was him respawning and coming back to raise the alarm. Getting to her feet SparkleGirl went quickly to the open doorway and listened. Thankfully no one came to find out the cause of the noise and commotion.

Now that plan A was sorted, it was time for plan B. Unfortunately SparkleGirl hadn't thought that far ahead. Even though that she was now free, she really wasn't, she had just gone from being in a small cell to now being in a bigger one. How was she going to get out of ChuckBone's fortress, she really didn't know right now. With that thought in mind, she slowly closed the cell door behind her and headed to the nearest door. It would probably only be a matter of time before ChuckBone would come looking for her, so it was best if she got quickly away from the cell block.

SparkleGirl opened the first door that she came to, and popped her head through for a quick peek. Thankfully the hall it lead onto was a quiet one without any players around. Then thinking it over SparkleGirl realised that, other than the players that had escorted her to her cell and ChuckBone, not many people knew her identity. If she wanted, she could get away with walking around in public without fear of being stopped. Her next objective was to get a weapon, walking around in public was one thing, walking around with no weapon to defend herself was a different matter.

Trying the first door knob she came to, she found herself in the room of her dreams. An armoury stocked with every type of weapon she could use, and much more. Other than a normal armoury that just contained swords, bows, arrows and axes, this was one also contain magical potions and even ender pearls. "One of the benefits of having a witch as a good pal," SparkleGirl thought to herself. Smiling to herself now, SparkleGirl realized that she was about to give ChuckBone a day he would remember for a long, long time.

Chapter 11

Looking around, SparkleGirl's head swam with excitement. Toughness potions, swiftness potions, regeneration potions, strength potions, healing potions, it was all here. To SparkleGirl this was like waking up on Christmas day and having Santa Claus leave all the worlds toys, just at your house.

"Where do I begin?" SparkleGirl asked herself. A bow and sword would have to be her first priority, along with as many arrows as she could carry. SparkleGirl took her time going through the weapon section, she'd probably be busy with a sword and bow, so she went for the best she could find. Picking out an enchanted bow and sword, SparkleGirl then decided on what potions she would choose. Moving along the potion shelf she quickly grabbed a strength, swiftness, healing, regeneration and invisibility potion followed by some ender pearls. Now having a well stock inventory SparkleGirl felt more confident of doing well in the upcoming fight.

Looking at the vast array of potions SparkleGirl knew that these would give ChuckBone a great advantage in his fight against Herobrine. This was something that couldn't be allowed to happen. Looking around SparkleGirl found just what she needed. There lying stacked against the back wall were TNT and fire chargers. SparkleGirl knew she'd better act fast; it wouldn't take long before they found her missing from her cell and come looking for her. Carrying as much TNT as she could at a time, she quickly placed the explosive charges all around the room and under the potions shelf.

SparkleGirl checked her inventory to make sure she had all she needed. There was no point in blowing up this room without first making sure she had everything she needed. Happy now that she was well equipped, SparkleGirl pulled out three fire chargers and placed them on three blocks of TNT. Then making sure they were lit, she ran for the door.

SparkleGirl knew she wouldn't have much time to get away once the TNT was lit, but where should she run to. Doing things properly would have meant going out, finding a safe exit, and then coming back to light the TNT. But what if she were captured on the way. This was something that she couldn't let happen. Running blindly up the hallway, she counted mentally in her head, any second now. Then just as she had been expecting, the explosives ripped through the building and sent debris flying in all directions. Knocked over by the force SparkleGirl found herself lying face down on the floor with her ears ringing. It would only be a matter of seconds now before they would come to check out the mess. Quickly grabbing the invisibility potion from her inventory she drank it down and waited.

Then just as she expected the first players came running to examine the damage. Standing back with her back flat against the wall, SparkleGirl moved slowly away from the scene. She knew though she was invisible she was vulnerable. While the potion worked a treat for her, she knew that any bow or sword she would carry in her hand would not be covered by it. Anyone seeing a floating weapon was bound to know where she was and attack it.

Holding her breath for fear of making noise, she saw the first player run past her with a shocked look on his face. "Oh, my God, the armoury, someone has blown the armoury" he cried out to the ones coming running behind. "What, how, who would have done this?" the second one asked. "Who was down here at the time?" another asked. "Just Jacklore, he was guarding that girl until ChuckBone had made up his mind with what to do with her!" "Quickly search her cell and find Jacklore," the leader called out. "ChuckBone's not going to be too happy when he sees this mess, and especially if it was that girl that caused it. I knew she was trouble from the moment I saw her, I'm just glad I got a chance to knock her out."

SparkleGirl knew she had to be fast. This invisibility potion wouldn't last for ever, and she didn't want to reappear in front of this crowd. Happy to know that her captors were running the wrong way, she jogged as quickly and quietly as she could in the opposite direction. Judging by what one of the players had said back there, ChuckBone was not back yet from his patrol or whatever he was on. She'd love to see the look on his face when he heard the news. Then again maybe he already knew. A huge explosion like that, and a large billow of smoke coming from his fortress would probably be seen and heard many miles away.

When SparkleGirl found her way out of the building her invisibility potion had already run out, but she wasn't worried now. Standing in the courtyard she found the whole place was in confusion with players wondering what had happened to their once safe home. This confusion gave SparkleGirl a chance to fit in without being noticed. Keeping to herself and trying to stay in the shadows, she thought it would be best if she could make her way to the front gate. Looking to the sky to calculate the time, she could see that the day was almost over, and darkness was starting to fall. Would this be the night Herobrine would attack, she wondered. She hoped so; she'd just given him a huge advantage in the battle, now that ChuckBone's armoury was destroyed. Maybe that was all the help she could give Herobrine in the fight.

Without waiting another moment, SparkleGirl raced to the front gate for her escape. But found it closely guarded and shut tight. ChuckBone's more experienced players had taken positions all around it, as a precaution to the explosion. Now patrolling with swords drawn, this was going to make SparkleGirl's chance of escape even harder. What could she do now she wondered? Before she had a chance to calculate a plan of action, she heard a shout from behind her.

"THERE SHE IS, THE ONE THAT CAUSED THE EXPLOSION. GET HER!" Turning around SparkleGirl looked to see the player who had knocked her out, come running in her direction with his sword held high. "Damn!" SparkleGirl said to herself. Moving quickly, she pulled her bow off her shoulder and put in her first arrow. Almost without looking, she immediately fired an arrow in his direction and watched as it hit him full in the chest. "THAT'S FOR HITTING A GIRL!" SparkleGirl called out, and then turned to find her next target.

Turning just in time she saw an arrow come straight for her head, which she barely avoided by diving to the ground. The players were coming in too close to use her bow anymore, and she couldn't fight hand to hand with what looked like ten players. Wondering what to do next, SparkleGirl pulled an Ender Pearl out of her inventory and fired it with all her strength at the high walkway above her. Almost instantly she teleported and found herself standing safely high above the group of players. "Where did she go?" one player asked looking around. He didn't get time to ask another question when SparkleGirl shot an arrow into his neck. "LOOK UP THERE. ON THE WALKWAY, GET HER," another player cried out.

Now that she had a second to catch her breath and thoughts, SparkleGirl wondered if it was wise what she was doing. Sure she could hold off for a while and kill some players, but what would be the use. For every player, she would kill they would only return to their bed, respawn and come back for more. Unless she could get out, this was a fight she could never win. That was unless she could destroy every bed in the fortress, which would be impossible. Then wondering what to do next she heard a cry from outside the wall.

"QUICKLY, OPEN THE GATE, WE'RE UNDER ATTACK!"

Chapter 12

"Oh, thank you Herobrine," SparkleGirl said looking up to the sky, he could've come at a better time. Standing on her toes to see better over the outer wall, SparkleGirl could see ChuckBone and his small gang of players come running towards the front gate. Then looking back to where one player was pointing, she could see Herobrine's army standing on the hill waiting for their instructions.

Looking back into the fortress SparkleGirl could see the place erupt into utter chaos and terror. The players that were after her, now changed their minds and were racing to get the front gate open for ChuckBone and his group. Time I was moving, SparkleGirl thought to herself. She knew that after the gate had closed, all attention would be back on her again. Better to run and hide while everyone was distracted. Herobrine might still need her help, and she couldn't afford to get killed and then respawn miles away from the battle.

Immediately after he came through the gate, ChuckBone's players sealed it and ran to meet him. "What happened?" ChuckBone cried. "I heard the explosion and saw the smoke and came as fast as I could. That was when we ran into that lot out there and barely made it away with our lives. Are we under attack already?" "No ChuckBone, it was that girl you caught, she escaped and blew our whole armoury to smithereens!"

"AAAARRGGGHHHH!" ChuckBone screamed. "YOU MEAN IT'S ALL GONE, EVERYTHING?" "I 'm sorry ChuckBone we tried our best, but she's escaped" "Escaped, where?" ChuckBone asked, grabbing the player by the collar and pulling him right up to his face. "She, she, I don't know where she is. Somewhere in the fortress." "You fools, one girl to look after, and you let her escape." Filled to the brim with anger now, ChuckBone pulled back his hand and punched the player square in the face, sending him falling to the ground.

"FIND HER!" he screamed to the other players around him. SparkleGirl watched as ChuckBone went to the middle of the courtyard, looked all around him and then roared at the top of his lungs, "SPARKLEGIRL, I KNOW YOU CAN HEAR ME. YOU'LL NEVER ESCAPE FROM

THIS PLACE ALIVE, I PROMISE YOU!" Listening from above, SparkleGirl could hear not only the anger but also the frustration in ChuckBone's voice. He'd made a mistake taking her into his fortress, and now he had paid for it. With his weapons and potions now gone, she could tell his confidence level had dropped dramatically.

Watching ChuckBone leave to make plans for the upcoming fight, SparkleGirl took this time to watch what Herobrine was getting up to. Looking down from the high wall she could make out his army in the twilight. Watching closely, she could see Herobrine's troop start to break into two groups. One group started to go to the left while the other group went to the right. He was planning on surrounding Chuckbone's fort. Looking at them move, SparkleGirl knew Herobrine would want to get this fight started and finished as soon as possible. Herobrine didn't have the luxury of being able to sit around for days at a time. He would strike hard, and strike fast while it was still dark.

SparkleGirl pulled her bow off her shoulder and thought through what she was about to do next. Happy with her plan, she took out a swiftness potion and drank it in one go. She would need speed right now. Climbing out from behind her hiding place, she ran along the walkway on the high wall and got her bow ready. If Herobrine were to stand any chance of getting near that wall, he would need help. Pulling out two arrows, she placed one in her bow and one between her teeth, and with quick succession fired them, hitting two players who had been guarding the wall. The first one dead on the spot immediately, while the second one went over the wall screaming to his death.

Even though she had a swiftness potion in her, SparkleGirl knew it would only be a matter of time before the other lookouts on the wall saw what she was doing. Grabbing another two arrows, she fired them off hitting one player in the neck and missing the second one, who had seen her coming. As she'd feared, her plan was now rumbled, and other players started to return fire with their bows. "SHES ON THE HIGH WALL, SHES ON THE HIGH WALL!" one player from below screamed and ran to the stairway to catch up with her. He never made it. Running past the top of the stairs, SparkleGirl fired an arrow down the stairway and hit him in the chest sending him falling backwards down the stairs with a loud clatter. She knew her luck wouldn't keep up but if she could spoil things long enough until Herobrine's attack, then that would be enough.

ChuckBone seeing what was happening, ran with a group of his players to give their support. "You fools don't let her escape. You're surrounded SparkleGirl give yourself up, you've nowhere to run to!" ChuckBone called out. "That's funny I was going to say the same thing to you," SparkleGirl remarked back. "Look outside ChuckBone. I think you're in more trouble than I am."

"You brought this Herobrine, here. This is your doing isn't it SparkleGirl?" ChuckBone asked coming slowly up the stairs with his sword drawn. "Actually it was YOU who brought him here ChuckBone. You're to blame for the mess you now find yourself in. You and that witch of yours," SparkleGirl said.

ChuckBone paused when he heard this. "Witch, what witch?" "You and I know, what witch. The one that's been giving you all the protection around here. The one that's given you all these potions that witch. But I wouldn't be waiting for her to come rescue you anytime soon ChuckBone. She's dead. Well she should be, because I chopped off her head," SparkleGirl said and started to laugh. When ChuckBone heard this, SparkleGirl could see his head drop a little more. He realized now that this was a battle he was going to have to fight all on his own.

"KILL HER!" ChuckBone roared to the players around him and stood back to let his cronies do his dirty work. SparkleGirl pulled out her sword and got ready for the fight. She had no hatred for these players or wanted to hurt them, but if they were going to put themselves between herself and ChuckBone they were going to go down. SparkleGirl lunged at the first player just as he got close to her. He had mistaken thought that she would go backwards rather than forwards and was caught off balance. SparkleGirl easily sliced through his sword arm, and both of them watched as his arm and sword fell with a clatter to the ground far below. The next player swung at her head but missed. SparkleGirl had seen what was coming, dropped to the ground and swung her sword hard. Her sword cut cleanly through the player's leg, which then set him off balance, and he fell to join the arm and sword on the ground below. After that the remaining players stood still.

"WHO'S NEXT?" SparkleGirl cried out and waved her sword in a threatening way towards them. Seeing the rage and skill that SparkleGirl had, they all stepped backwards. "LOOK AT YOUR GREAT LEADER NOW!" SparkleGirl said and pointed to ChuckBone, who was now making a hasty retreat to the safety of a building. "Do you really want to die for someone like him?" SparkleGirl watched as the players thought about it, and then stopped in their tracks. "I thought so!" Grabbing an Ender pearl from her inventory, SparkleGirl fired it to the ground and teleported there. There was no way ChuckBone was escaping her now. Knowing him he'd have an escape tunnel or some other way to get out of here. But that wasn't going to happen, not if she had anything to do with it.

Now that everyone's attention was distracted by SparkleGirl's exit. They never noticed the first spider come over the wall until it was too late. Grabbing one stunned player it tossed him easily backwards over the wall to his death. Herobrine's battle had finally begun.

Chapter 13

Once the wall was breached by the first spider, it was plain to see how many experienced players ChuckBone "really" had. Running to meet the threat a small group of players fought off the spider quickly and moved on to face a group of zombies that had come in through a huge hole blown in the wall. Now that Herobrine had the walls, he was free to send in whatever he wanted. Moving as many spiders as he could, he sent them in from all sides. Then when all the lookouts were busy or killed, he sent creepers in groups of three, to blow themselves up against the wall. These deadly explosion left huge holes in the walls where zombies, creepers and skeletons were free to do as they pleased.

*****

SparkleGirl stopped in her tracks when she heard the first explosion. She knew Herobrine now had his foot in the door; it would only be a matter of time before the fortress fell to him. Looking to the source of the explosion, she could now see skeletons come running through the cloud of dust. Once inside they easily picked off some of the noob players with their arrows. Looking at what was happening in front of her SparkleGirl felt sorry for those players. They had made a mistake tying themselves to ChuckBone and now they had paid for it. But that was life in Minecraft, you made mistakes, made the wrong decisions, got killed, came back and moved on. She knew all too well, what that was like.

Pushing aside all those thoughts to concentrate on what her real mission was, SparkleGirl continued running in the direction ChuckBone had gone. Once inside the building and not knowing what was ahead of her, she slowed her pace. Where could a no good coward like him be hiding, she wondered to herself. Pulling her sword out she held it tightly and walked onwards. If she knew ChuckBone, which she did, he wouldn't leave himself alone to face her, he'd have back up. Then turning the next corner she met it.

Standing in the narrow hallway, she found two players blocking her way ahead. Knowing that these two were put there to slow her down, rather than as protection for ChuckBone, she swore to herself. Looking at the two of them she politely asked, "Would you two gents, please move out of my way. I've an important matter to see to with ChuckBone?" On hearing this the two players looked at each other and laughed. "I think he's too busy at the moment. Maybe we can help," one of them asked. "I really don't want to hurt you two guys. So this is my last warning, move aside," SparkleGirl said and put away her sword. When the players saw this move, they both sneered and laughed, "So we've captured the "great" SparkleGirl. Too much of a match for you, were we." "Not really!" SparkleGirl said and flicked an Ender Pearl over their shoulders. As soon as she teleported behind them, SparkleGirl instantly pulled out her sword and swung it with great force, leaving the players bodies to fall without any heads.

Kneeling on the ground now, SparkleGirl could feel a great weakness in her. Those three teleportation's had taken a lot from her health bar, and she needed to replenish it. Reaching into her inventory, she took out a regeneration potion and drank it down in one gulp. Once it entered her stomach and bloodstream she could feel it doing its work. Where once she had been tired and sore, she now felt like she had stepped into a brand new body. Swinging her sword to admire how great she now felt, she ran on again in the chase after ChuckBone.

SparkleGirl hoped that the fight she had had with those two players would be the only one she would have on the way to ChuckBone. Each one would just be another waste of time and let him get further away from her grasp. She wondered if he did have an escape tunnel. Surely someone like ChuckBone, who had great confidence in the strength of his home, would still build an escape tunnel. No one could be that stupid, could they? Then turning the next corner and entering a large room, she got her answer.

Standing in front of her holding a sword was ChuckBone along with his two of his closest friends. The ones who had killed her so very long ago. "Surprised to see you still here ChuckBone?" SparkleGirl said. "I thought you'd have been long gone, like a rat running away in your tunnel. But I was wrong. You'd so much faith in that witch of yours that you thought she'd come in here and save you, didn't you?" "The only one needing saving today is you SparkleGirl!" ChuckBone snarled back. "Maybe you've not seen what's been going on outside ChuckBone. The last I saw, your precious fortress was being taken apart by Herobrine, and your players were fleeing for their lives. That doesn't sound like a man who's winning," SparkleGirl sneered back.

"Get her. It's because of her, that Herobrine is here. Once we have her, we can make a trade. Her life for his surrender," ChuckBone said with a grin. Feeling more confident by this idea, he pushed the two players forward in front of him. "Don't let her get away this time," ChuckBone snapped at them. SparkleGirl watched as the two players started to come at her, now moving apart from each other so that they could attack from both sides. Back when she'd originally known these two, she'd been nothing more than a noob with very little battle experience. But now things were a whole lot different.

Pretending to be afraid of what was going to happen, SparkleGirl moved backwards. She knew a move like this would be read as fear, and give them more confidence. This is what she wanted. Looking at the two players, she picked one and ran at him. Caught by surprise and off balance the player swung his sword where her head had been and missed. SparkleGirl dived safely under the oncoming sword and curled in a ball. Now that she was behind him, she turned, swung her sword, and cut him deeply across the back. One down, one to go, SparkleGirl thought to herself.

Smiling at the other player SparkleGirl could see he had underestimated her skill. He'd assumed that she was still the noob he'd known. "Do you want to get hurt for him?" SparkleGirl asked pointing to ChuckBone. "Believe me, he's so not worth it. If you want to leave now, that's fine with me. This fight is between me and ChuckBone." Looking from SparkleGirl to ChuckBone and back again, the player stepped backwards and threw his sword at SparkleGirl's feet.

ChuckBone watched in surprise as his once close friend ran away in retreat. "YOU COWARD, I'LL HUNT YOU DOWN LIKE A DOG AFTER THIS!" ChuckBone screamed after him. "I think you're forgetting something ChuckBone. You have to escape from me first!" SparkleGirl said smiling at him. "I won't fight a girl," ChuckBone said. "You'll have to, because there's no way you're leaving this room alive unless you do," SparkleGirl replied loosing up her sword arm. "Please SparkleGirl whatever it was that I'd done to you, I'm sorry" ChuckBone told her in a whimpering voice. "If, for a second, I did believe you I'd be letting you go," SparkleGirl said not taking her eye off him.

At that ChuckBone put away his sword and held his two hands up as a sign of surrender. Looking at this SparkleGirl wondered what to do next. Could she really cut down an unarmed player? She wanted revenge, but this wasn't the right way to do it. Maybe it was best to let Herobrine sort this problem out. Then just when she had relaxed herself out of her fighting stance, she saw the quick movement of ChuckBone's hand.

She knew what was going to happen next but was too slow to react. Almost instantly after she saw the Ender pearl go past her, she then felt ChuckBone's sword on her throat. "You should have killed me when you had the chance," ChuckBone sneered into her ear. "I guessssss I win again," he said in an almost snake-like fashion. "It has been nice to see again, but now I really must say goodbye." Closing her eyes tightly, SparkleGirl prepared herself for death. It would only be a matter of time before she would respawn out of this place. She had done her best, but unfortunately ChuckBone had got the better of her again.

Then without warning she heard a piercing scream in her ear, followed by ChuckBone's sword clattering to the ground. Surprised SparkleGirl quickly turned to see Herobrine standing with a bloody axe in his hand. Now looking down SparkleGirl could see the reason for ChuckBone's scream. There lying on the ground was ChuckBone's severed arm still holding onto his sword. "Herobrine, please don't kill me. This wasn't my doing, it was the witch. She was the one behind all of this," ChuckBone pleaded and tried to move away from Herobrine. Looking at Herobrine's face, SparkleGirl couldn't tell what emotions must be going through his mind. As always his face was a mask that was unreadable. But his eyes, were different. Although they usually burned brightly, they burned now with a white intensity she'd never seen before.

As ChuckBone pleaded again for his life, Herobrine stepped to the side. Now SparkleGirl could see what he'd brought with him. There standing behind him were three very large spiders. With a quick nod of his head, Herobrine released them at ChuckBone. Instantly the three spiders leapt onto the screaming ChuckBone and torn into his body pulling it between them. At this SparkleGirl turned away from the gruesome sight. This was something she'd want to see.

When she opened her eyes again, she found Herobrine standing in front her. Startled that she'd not heard him come up beside her, she jumped a little. Then wondering what was about to happen next she saw him raise his hand to her face. Holding his hand there and looking into his eyes she could see that whatever fury had been there, was now gone. "I'm sorry," she said." I know now I can never change things. Please forgive me!" By the way, he looked at her; SparkleGirl could see he had peace in him now. All the loose ends had finally been tied up. ChuckBone was gone, the witch who'd controlled him was dead and finally he was free of it all. Then taking his hand away from her face, he nodded and disappeared.

Now in a daze at what had happened, SparkleGirl turned to find herself completely alone. Herobrine was gone, and so too were ChuckBone's body and the three large spiders. Picking up her sword and putting it away SparkleGirl walked back out into the large courtyard and looked up into the sky. The sun was starting to rise, and it felt like she'd been born again. Gone were all those feelings of revenge and pain that she'd once felt. Today it felt like it was going to be the first day in a wonderful new life for her.

Chapter 14

It had been two months since the great battle at ChuckBone's fortress. Over those two months, the whole Minecraft world was fuelled with rumour and speculation about what had happened. Some people said that they had been there and saw Herobrine shoots bolts of fire from his mouth. While others said that he grew to over twenty times his size and stamped on fleeing players. That was life in Minecraft, everyone trying to outdo each other with their tall tales. But there was one thing for sure, no one even SparkleGirl really knew where Herobrine was now. Maybe he'd killed himself, now that his mission in life was over. He'd gotten his revenge on ChuckBone, maybe that enough for him and he just wanted to be left alone. Who knew, but she hoped that at last he was at peace now, and his fighting days were over.

Like Herobrine, SparkleGirl's life was never the same again. After the fight, she'd made her way back home and rebuilt it. But although her home was back to normal, her life now was far different. Good ole BuckSeth good to his word had told everyone he knew about the link between SparkleGirl and Herobrine. Of course, it was not the truth but an exaggeration of the events that had happened and her life had suffered for it. No longer could she travel through an area anymore without people talking behind her back and pointing. Like Herobrine, she had now become an outsider in the Minecraft world.

But while this had given her great pain in the beginning, it had also given her great protection. No longer would anyone dare to attack her for fear that Herobrine could come back for revenge. She smiled at this and scratched Wolfie2 under the chin. It was so good to have him back by her side. Leaving the destroyed fortress that day, she'd thought she would never see him again. But on walking back to where she'd been captured, she found him curled up asleep in the pit she'd made. He had waited there patiently for her to come back. Deep down inside he knew that she would.

Putting her arm around her loveable dog, the two of them watched the setting sun go down. "Ready to go inside for the night boy?" SparkleGirl asked. "I think I *just* might have a juicy steak in the kitchen?" Wolfie2 licked his lips and barked in delight. "It's the least I could do for you, after all you've done for me. You big hairy beast!" With that SparkleGirl, ran off laughing before he could react. "Last one home doesn't get any steak!" SparkleGirl shouted back over her shoulder.

Wolfie2 jumped to his feet and ran after her barking; this was one race he wasn't going to lose.

The End.

Herobrine – Revenge of a Monster Now On Audiobook

Now Available on Audible.com and iTunes

Bonus Chapters from SparkleGirl – Trained By a Monster.

Chapter 1

"A pleasure to meet you again SparkleGirl. You probably don't remember me but I definitely remember you. How could I ever forget the person who killed me? But then again, you did do a lot of killing that day. Now let's see how great, the great SparkleGirl is without Herobrine by her side."

Chapter 2

Seven days earlier...

Wiping the sweat from her brow SparkleGirl stood back to admire her handiwork. "Well, what do you think boy?" SparkleGirl asked looking over at her dog. Wolfie2 snorted back in response and then yawned. "Not impressed?" she asked. "I'd like to see any hostile mob break through those defences."

Turning her attention back to what she'd built, SparkleGirl wondered if those extra defences were really needed anymore. Things weren't as bad as they'd been, now that Herobrine was gone. His disappearance and the witch that had controlled him seemed to leave a gap in the evilness that there had been in Minecraft. But SparkleGirl knew that that would change, ChuckBone had been evidence of that. He'd once been a normal player but his lust for power and greed had brought misery to so many players in Minecraft. You thought you were invincible ChuckBone, but you didn't count on Herobrine, did you, SparkleGirl thought and smiled.

SparkleGirl knew it would only be a matter of time before someone else filled the vacuum ChuckBone had left, but she didn't care. As long as they stayed out of her way and didn't bring trouble to her front door they could do what they wanted. "Time to call it a day boy," SparkleGirl said to Wolfie2. "I promise tomorrow things will be different. I know how bored you've been hanging around here with me. So let's make tomorrow a day just for you. What do you say?" Wolfie2 barked excitedly in response. "It's a date then, you big hairy hound," SparkleGirl said and ruffled the fur on

Wolfie2's head. Thinking her plan over a day spend hunting little piggies and using her bow sounded like bliss right now. "Come on boy let's get that furnace fired up and get some foo…" But before SparkleGirl had a chance to say anything more Wolfie2 was gone, running at full speed in the direction of the kitchen.

Taking a moment to admire the setting sun SparkleGirl wondered what tomorrow would bring. You could never really tell in Minecraft, its randomness along with its beauty was something she enjoyed about the game. Then that was like life in the real world too, who knew what surprise was waiting for you around the corner. Lost in her thoughts SparkleGirl was drawn back to the real world when she heard Wolfie2 barking at her. "Oh yeah, sorry boy I'm coming. I was just thinking about something for a moment. How about we get some of that fine steak and potatoes out for tonight's meal, I think we deserve it."

Clearing up after supper SparkleGirl went over what she would need for the next day's hunting. Filling her inventory with plenty of arrows and snacks, she then tested the string on her bow. Maybe it's better if I bring two with me, she thought to herself. The last thing she needed was to end her days hunting because of a broken bow. It wouldn't be the end of the world and she could of course resort to killing her prey with a sword, but where was the fun in that. Anyone could kill with a sword up close, but it took skill to kill your prey from a distance with a bow.

Happy that she'd everything sorted for her next day's hunting, SparkleGirl patrolled her home one last time before bedtime. She knew it probably wasn't needed, but you could never be too safe in Minecraft. The last thing you wanted was to find a hostile mob in an exit tunnel, or not have a weapon close at hand when you really needed it. Then it was game over because of a stupid mistake, something SparkleGirl didn't want to die from.

Satisfied that her home was secure for the night, SparkleGirl called for Wolfie2. "Come on boy, we've got an early rise in the morning and you'll need your beauty sleep." SparkleGirl smiled as she watched Wolfie2 run on ahead of her to get to her bed before she did. "You better make room for me, you hairy hound. It's just for tonight OK. Tomorrow you're back to sleeping in your own bed." Wolfie2 turned his head when he heard this and let out a snort of disgust. "Same to you, now push over!" SparkleGirl said and pushed her dog over to one side to make some room in her bed.

Waking the next morning, SparkleGirl went up to her perimeter wall and looked out at the world beyond it. Last night had been another quiet night with very little activity from hostile mobs. She was grateful for this and stretched to loosen up the tight muscles in her back, which came from the previous days digging and the lack of room in her bed that night. Looking off toward the horizon she could see the cubic sun was just starting to make its way skyward. It was time to get moving. Leaving her high lookout position SparkleGirl walked to her kitchen and quickly prepared some pork chops for breakfast. It would be a long day.

*****

Standing outside her front gate SparkleGirl laughed at the spectacle Wolfie2 was putting on. Excited that he was going outside for the whole day, Wolfie2 started limbering up and stretching the sleep out of his body. Then when he was ready he took off without any notice. "WAIT FOR ME YOU FOOL!" SparkleGirl roared after her dog and sprinted to keep up with him. There was always one thing that she could depend on and that was Wolfie2's nose. Whatever scent he had just picked up, he was now very keen on catching up with its owner.

Two hours later SparkleGirl stood at the top of a hill and tried to catch her breath. Today's hunting had been a great success and they'd done well. Looking down from her high view point she could see the local village below in the distance. That was where she wanted to keep it. People from the village avoided her now because of her friendship with Herobrine. She couldn't blame them. If she was in their position would she trust someone who was a friend to a monster like that? She didn't think so. But then they didn't know or even care, that she'd known him when he was just an ordinary player. Small minded people in a small minded town, SparkleGirl thought to herself. Then throwing that thought to the back of her mind, SparkleGirl looked around her to see what Wolfie2 was getting up to. Running on ahead to catch up with him she found him standing motionless looking down at a group of players below him. "What is it boy, what have you found?" SparkleGirl asked. Looking to where her dog was gazing, she knew to be quiet. Lying down on her belly SparkleGirl crawled forward to hear what the players were saying.

Find Out What Happens Next In…

Available In All Online Bookstores

Thanks

Thanks for purchasing a copy of Herobrine – Revenge of a Monster. If you enjoyed the book, please take a moment to leave a review. It's greatly appreciated and helps to get this book in front of more new readers.

Thank you.

Barry J McDonald

Why not drop by my Facebook page and "Like It"

https://www.facebook.com/BarrysMinecraftNovels

www.MinecraftNovels.com

Printed in Great Britain
by Amazon.co.uk, Ltd.,
Marston Gate.